Traction Man
Is Here!

MINI GREY

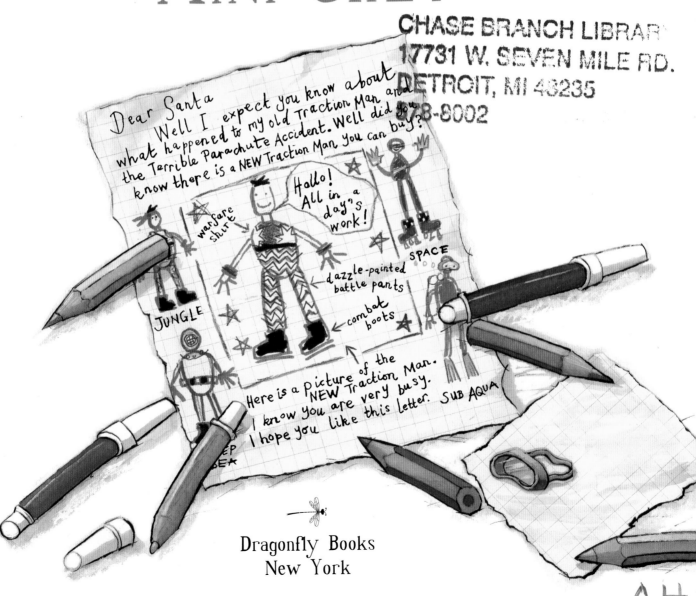

Dear Santa
Well I expect you know about what happened to my old Traction Man and the Terrible Parachute Accident. Well did you know there is a NEW Traction Man you can buy?

Hollo! All in a day's work!

warfare shirt

dazzle-painted battle pants

combat boots

JUNGLE

SPACE

Here is a picture of the NEW Traction Man. I know you are very busy. I hope you like this letter. SUB AQUA

Dragonfly Books
New York

Traction Man is guarding some toast.

Now who's going to help with the washing up?

He volunteers for a Special Mission.

Traction Man is diving in the foamy waters
of the Sink (wearing his Sub-Aqua Suit,
Fluorescent Flippers, and Infra-Red Mask).

He is searching for the
Lost Wreck of the Sieve.

"Well done,
    Scrubbing Brush!
        You can be my pet!"

Just ten minutes, remember...

Traction Man is crawling through the overgrown shrubbery near the Pond, wearing Jungle Pants, Camouflage Vest and Sweaty Bandanna.

The Dollies have all been buried up to their waists in the flowerbed by Wicked Professor Spade.

"Oh, Traction Man, how can we repay you?"
"Think nothing of it, Ladies.
                    All in a day's work."

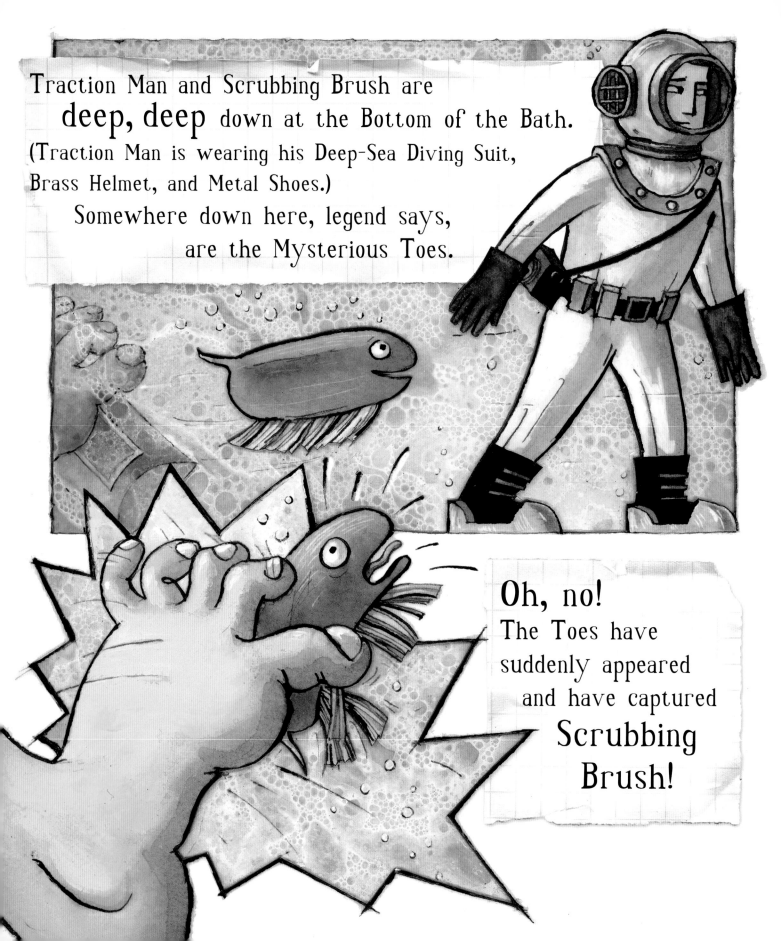

Traction Man and Scrubbing Brush are **deep, deep** down at the Bottom of the Bath.
(Traction Man is wearing his Deep-Sea Diving Suit, Brass Helmet, and Metal Shoes.)

Somewhere down here, legend says, are the Mysterious Toes.

Oh, no!
The Toes have suddenly appeared and have captured **Scrubbing Brush!**

"No Mysterious Toes can steal away with my brave pet! **Take that!** **And that!**"

The Toes cannot **stand** it and release Scrubbing Brush.

Traction Man takes some photographs of the Mysterious Toes.

Traction Man and Scrubbing Brush are in the Giant InterGalactic People Mover.

They are counting Christmas trees.

They are put into suspended animation for some of the journey.

At last!
Granny's!

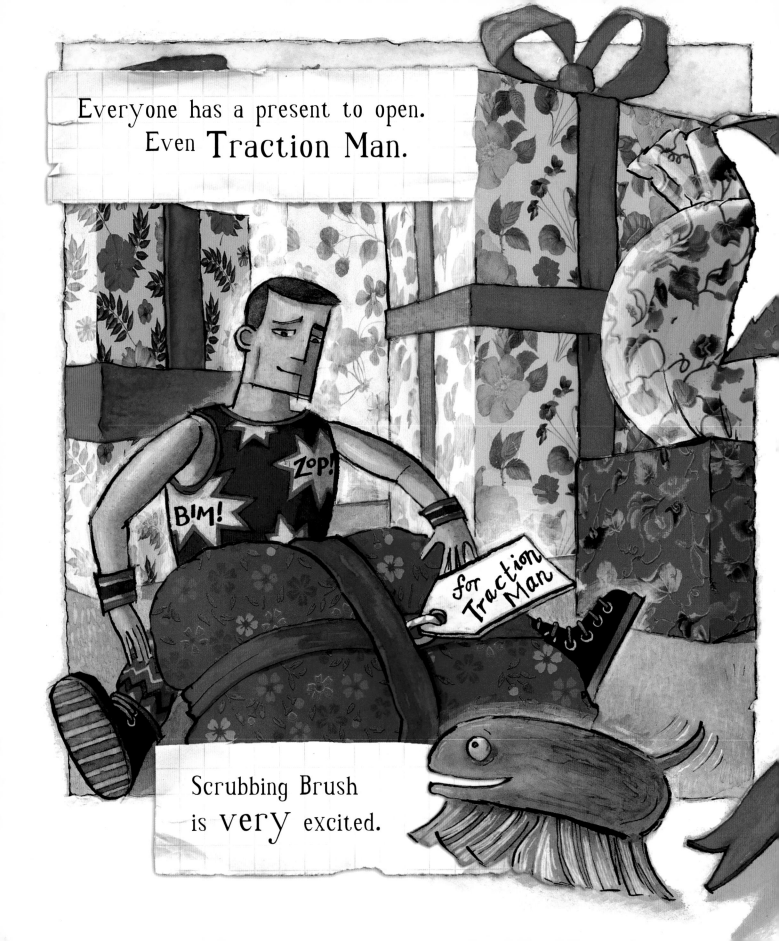

Everyone has a present to open.
Even Traction Man.

Scrubbing Brush
is very excited.

Oh! How lovely (grrrr).
An all-in-one knitted green romper suit
and matching bonnet!

It is a perfect fit.

Traction Man is sitting on the edge of the Kitchen Cliff (wondering how long he will have to wear his all-in-one knitted green romper suit and matching bonnet).

My goodness! Down there!
   All those Spoons have crashed! They must be helped—
but how? The Kitchen Cliff is very high.

Traction Man and **Scrubbing Brush**
are relaxing after their latest mission,
lying comfortably on a book
in the huge blue expanse
of the Carpet.

Traction Man is wearing his
knitted Green Swimming Pants
and matching Swimming Bonnet.

They are both wearing their medals.

And they know they are ready
for **Anything.**

To my
big brother
TONY

Copyright © 2005 by Mini Grey

Dragonfly Books with the colophon is a registered trademark of Random House, Inc.

Visit us on the Web! randomhouse.com/kids

Educators and librarians, for a variety of teaching tools, visit us at randomhouse.com/teachers

The Library of Congress has cataloged the hardcover edition of this work as follows:
Grey, Mini.
Traction Man is here! / by Mini Grey.
p. cm.
Summary: Traction Man, a boy's courageous action figure, has a variety of adventures with
Scrubbing Brush and other objects in the house.
ISBN 978-0-375-83191-1 (trade) — ISBN 978-0-375-93191-8 (lib. bdg.) —
ISBN 978-0-375-98701-4 (ebook)
[1. Action figures (Toys)—Fiction. 2. Toys—Fiction. 3. Brooms and brushes—Fiction.] I. Title.
PZ7.G873Tr 2005
[E]—dc22
2004004452

ISBN 978-0-307-93111-5 (pbk.)

MANUFACTURED IN SINGAPORE

10 9 8 7 6 5 4 3 2 1

First Dragonfly Books Edition